I'm a
LEPRECHAUN

By Mallory C. Loehr
Illustrated by Brian Biggs

A GOLDEN BOOK • NEW YORK

Text copyright © 2021 by Mallory C. Loehr.
Cover art and interior illustrations copyright © 2021 by Brian Biggs.
All rights reserved. Published in the United States by Golden Books, an imprint of Random House
Children's Books, a division of Penguin Random House LLC, 1745 Broadway, New York, NY 10019.
Golden Books, A Golden Book, A Little Golden Book, the G colophon, and the distinctive gold spine
are registered trademarks of Penguin Random House LLC.
rhcbooks.com
Educators and librarians, for a variety of teaching tools, visit us at RHTeachersLibrarians.com
Library of Congress Control Number: 2019943009
ISBN 978-0-593-12773-5 (trade) — ISBN 978-0-593-12774-2 (ebook)
Printed in the United States of America
10 9 8 7 6 5 4 3 2 1

I'm a
LEPRECHAUN.

Green suit, red hair, pointy ears,
and beard—that's me!

I live in Ireland,
a land of green and
rain and rainbows.

"Leprechaun" means "small body" in Irish, but we are taller than our cousins—the pixies, the fairies, and the elves.

Not many people know this, but leprechauns are wonderful shoemakers! If you're ever looking for me, listen for the *tap-tap-tap* of my hammer.

Which shoe do you like best?

I eat potatoes, mushrooms, and nuts. But wildflower stew is my favorite.

Leprechauns like
to be alone—

maybe because humans are
always chasing us for our gold!

I keep my gold in a pot that I hide
at the end of the rainbow.

If you catch me, I'll grant you three wishes or share my pot of gold. But watch out—I can be tricky. Just when you think you have me . . .

. . . I can disappear into the misty green forests where I live.

If you are kind, I might stick around and reward you.

I'm magical. I'm mischievous.
I'm the luck of the Irish!

I'm a LEPRECHAUN!

Catch me if you can!